→ This journal belongs to
Spark Elf.

If found, return
immediately
to the North Pole.

Please and Thank You.

Memoirs of an ELF

By Devin Scillian and Illustrated by Tim Bowers

Sleeping Bear Press™

315 East Eisenhower Parkway, Suite 200
Ann Arbor, MI 48108
www.sleepingbearpress.com

Printed and bound in the United States.

10 9 8 7 6 5 4 3 2 1

Library of Congress Cataloging-in-Publication Data

Scillian, Devin.
Memoirs of an elf / written by Devin Scillian ;
illustrated by Tim Bowers.
pages cm
Summary: "Under Spark Elf's direction, Santa delivers presents in the
allotted twenty-four hours only to arrive at the North Pole with a
stowaway in the toy bag, a family's beloved dog"-- Provided by the publisher.
ISBN 978-1-58536-910-2
[1. Elves--Fiction. 2. Santa Claus--Fiction. 3. Christmas--Fiction.]
I. Bowers, Tim, illustrator. II. Title.
PZ7.S41269Mg 2014
[E]--dc23
2014004556

Christmas Eve, 9:45 PM

Two hours until launch on Christmas Eve.

The sleigh is loaded, and I feel great!

My ears are nice and pointy, and I'm feeling extra short today!

Bobbin and Nutshell look really good, too.

Around the world in 24 hours, and it's our job to keep Santa on schedule.

I feel so good I snap an elfie.

10:45 PM

One hour before launch and it begins to snow.
The reindeer love it! We elves have a saying:
"No snow, no Christmas." But at the North Pole, it has
snowed every Christmas Eve for, like, 600 years so no
problem. I send a text to Santa: "Time to fly, big guy!"
He says I worry too much. He's probably right.

Little-known fact: Santa is a really smart guy.

Midnight

Launch time. Santa kisses Momma Claus and waves to the other elves.
I've got the GPS. Bobbin is in charge of the toy bag. And Nutshell has the Nice List.

Little-known fact: We don't even bring the Naughty List with us.

A crack of the whip and away we go into the polar sky.

I start the timer: 24 hours to go!

22 hours to go

So far, so good. Guam and Fiji were a little warm, but back up above the clouds we're as cool as popsicles as we head for New Zealand. Santa is singing "Here Comes Santa Claus."

Little-known fact: It's his favorite carol.

No music, no Christmas.

That's what I always say.

18 hours to go

Starting to worry about falling behind.
Santa always wants to stop and pet EVERY dog.

Little-known fact: Santa loves dogs and dogs love Santa.

He's playing with a dog named Tugboat when I yell down the chimney,
"Santa, we gotta go!" Santa just laughs like he always does.

12 hours to go, halfway around the world

Bobbin and Nutshell are arguing about whether the bag is half-full or half-empty.

We're falling further behind because the kids have left more cookies than usual this year. Santa tries to eat all of them, except ginger snaps.

Little-known fact: Santa doesn't like ginger snaps so he gives all of those to me, Bobbin, and Nutshell.

Little-known fact number two: You should leave ginger snaps for Santa. Please and thank you.

9 hours to go

We're really slow getting out of Mexico City. Kids there leave tamales for Santa and he loves tamales as much as cookies. I point to my watch and say, "Come on, big guy. No Santa, no Christmas!"

Santa just laughs and says, "Not true, Spark. I'll bet you a candy cane."

Little-known fact: When Santa is serious about something, he bets you a candy cane.

4 hours to go

We made up time in Brazil, but now Santa is taking too long again.
This time he's playing with a train set that he just delivered.
We're waiting so long that the reindeer start nibbling on some tinsel.
"NO!" I yell.

Little-known fact: Reindeer LOVE tinsel but it makes
them hyper. It's like 50 cups of coffee.

Bobbin drags Santa away
from the train set.

30 minutes to go

With all of the toys gone, the sleigh is very light now, and it's a good thing because the reindeer are exhausted. Santa pokes his head out of the last chimney and yells, "Merry Christmas to all, and to all a good night!"

We made it with half an hour to spare!

Little-known fact: At the last house, we always join hands and sing "Silent Night." The reindeer, too.

And we head for home.

The North Pole

Ta-da! We've done it again! Around the world in one night and we made it to every house! We land at the North Pole where everyone is there to greet us. There's singing and dancing and lots of hot chocolate. Oh, and French toast.

But as we're unloading the sleigh,
Bobbin says he doesn't think the toy bag is empty.
How can that be? We gave away every present on the list.
But it's not a present in the bag, and it just licked Bobbin's ear.

It's Tugboat!

"Ho! Ho! Ho! We have a stowaway!" laughs Santa as Tugboat covers his face in kisses. Santa is laughing and smiling, but I am not laughing. I'm panicking. "Santa," I say, "we stole someone's dog!"

The music stops, and everyone is quiet.

This has never happened before. Momma Claus says what everyone is thinking. "I don't think it's a very good Christmas morning at Tugboat's house."

Well-known fact: Santa gives things away.
He does not take things!

We are in ginormous trouble.

"Any ideas?" asks Santa.

Bobbin says we should put Tugboat in a box and mail him home.

Nutshell says we should keep Tugboat for a year and take him back next Christmas.

I suggest we put Tugboat in a hot air balloon and that he would probably mostly sort of be okay.

Momma Claus is the only one thinking clearly. **"Get back in the sleigh!"** she yells.

But the sun is just coming up.

Little-known fact: We have never flown during the day. People could see us!

We put sunglasses on the reindeer and change into disguises that probably aren't very good.

The reindeer are tired and confused, but Santa gives them a few nibbles of tinsel and they race for the runway. Suddenly we're off like a rocket back into the sky.

We're all very worried, except Tugboat.
He's having the ride of his life.

9:00 AM Christmas morning

We land behind some trees near Tugboat's house. Bobbin and Nutshell stay with Tugboat while Santa and I creep up to the window. It's worse than we thought.

There are all of the presents we brought, but they haven't been touched. Three children are crying. Their mother is on the phone, and their father is standing in the doorway yelling, **"Tugboat! Tugboat! HEEEERE, boy!"**

"How dreadful," whispers Santa. We sneak back to the sleigh.

Now it gets complicated. Bobbin thinks we should sneak Tugboat down the chimney. Nutshell is thinking about a big slingshot. I'm wondering if the back door is open. It seems impossible, really. But Santa gives Tugboat a pat and says, "Go ahead, boy." In a flash, Tugboat takes off like a rabbit through the trees, plowing through the snow and toward the house.

All of a sudden, the whole family is in a pile covering Tugboat
with hugs and kisses. More tears now, but they're the good kind.
And I have honestly never seen a happier family on Christmas morning.

Santa looks at me and smiles.

"No Tugboat, no Christmas," he says.

He's right. Of course, he's right.

I slide a candy cane from my pocket and hand it to Santa as we climb
back into the sleigh.

Little-known fact: Santa is a really smart guy.

We're really happy, and before we head for home, we snap an elfie.

Have a Merry Christmas.

Please and thank you.